CW00853196

Pinny's Party

Peter Firmin

ANDRE DEUTSCH

For Ruth, Elis and Meirion

Pinny and Victor are tiny 'Dutch' dolls, jointed wooden dolls made in Europe in many sizes since the eighteenth century.

After mending a very old and precious little doll, known as "The Smallest Doll in the World", Peter Firmin made this pair of dolls using a piece of wood from a holly tree.

Other Pinny stories to look out for are:
Pinny Finds A House, Pinny and the Bird,
Pinny in the Snow *and* Pinny and the Floppy Frog.

In a little china house on a shelf
in the sitting room lives a tiny
wooden doll, no taller than a pin,
and her name is Pinny.

Beside the house on the shelf
stands a toy sailing boat.
The smallest wooden sailor in
the world sits in the boat.
His name is Victor.

Pinny and Victor saw a butterfly on the curtain above the window sill. "I thought butterflies had pretty wings," said Pinny. "Why is it so dull?" "It's asleep," said Victor. "When it wakes up, it will open its wings. Then you'll see how pretty it is."

The children who play with the dolls are called Jo and Tom. They had left some things on the window sill; one of Jo's hairslides; some wrapped sweets; and Tom's clip-on bow tie. Pinny didn't know it was a bow tie. She thought it was another butterfly.

"Now that is a pretty butterfly," she said.
"Oh no," said Victor. "That's Tom's bow tie. They've been to a party."
"Shall we have a party?" said Pinny.
"Yes," said Victor. "We could dance and play games."

They had their party next morning,
before anybody was awake.
Victor managed to turn on the radio,
so they even had music.
"What's our party for?" asked Pinny.
"Oh, I don't know," said Victor.
"We'll think of something later."

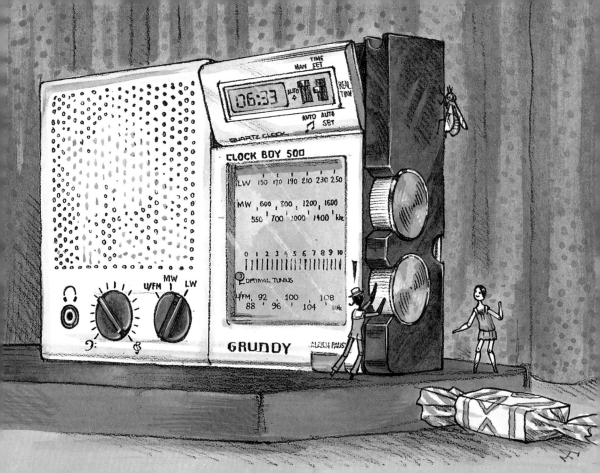

"We must dress up," said Pinny.
"But we haven't got any party
clothes," said Victor.
Pinny unwrapped some paper from
the sweets. "Now we have," she said.
They put on the sticky sweet papers.

Pinny and Victor played "Musical Chair".
Well, there were only two of them,
so one chair was enough.
Victor missed the chair and fell
on the floor with a BUMP!
So Pinny won that game.

Then Pinny hid a bead in a crumpled-up piece of paper and they played "Pass-the-Parcel". Victor found the bead, so he won that game.

Then they danced to the music. They danced on and on until they were quite puffed out. They sat down for a rest. A bright ray of sunshine shone through the curtain and warmed the sleeping butterfly.

The butterfly woke up, opened its wings and flew to the window, where it flapped against the glass, trying to get out into the warm sunshine.

"You see," said Victor. "It IS pretty, isn't it?"

"Now we know what the party was for," laughed Pinny. "It was a 'Butterfly-waking-up-Party'."

"So it was," said Victor.

The door opened and mum came into the room.

"Who left the radio on?" she said, "and who's been eating sweets and left the papers all over the place!" She was just about to brush Pinny and Victor away with the sweet papers when she saw the butterfly at the window.

"Oh, the poor creature," she said. And, very carefully, so as not to damage its wings, she caught the butterfly and took it outside. She opened her hands and it flew away into the sunshine.

While she was outside, Pinny and Victor took off their party clothes. When mum came back she was surprised to see them sitting there. She picked them up, wiped them, and put them back on the shelf.

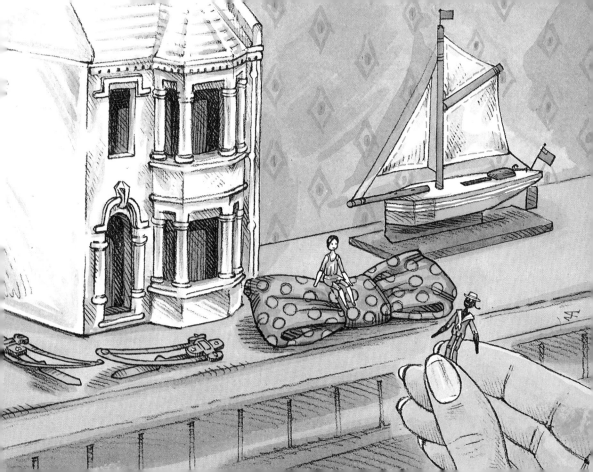

"My goodness," she said, "how sticky
you were. It's lucky I found you.
Something terrible might have happened."

First published in 1987 by
André Deutsch Limited
105-106 Great Russell Street London WC1B 3LJ
Copyright © 1987 By Peter Firmin
All rights reserved
Printed in Great Britain by Cambus Litho

British Library Cataloguing in Publication Data

Firmin, Peter
  Pinny's party.
  I. Title
  823' .914 [J]   PZ7
   ISBN 0-233-97857-7